UNDERWEAR!

By Jenn Harney

Disney • HYPERION
Los Angeles   New York

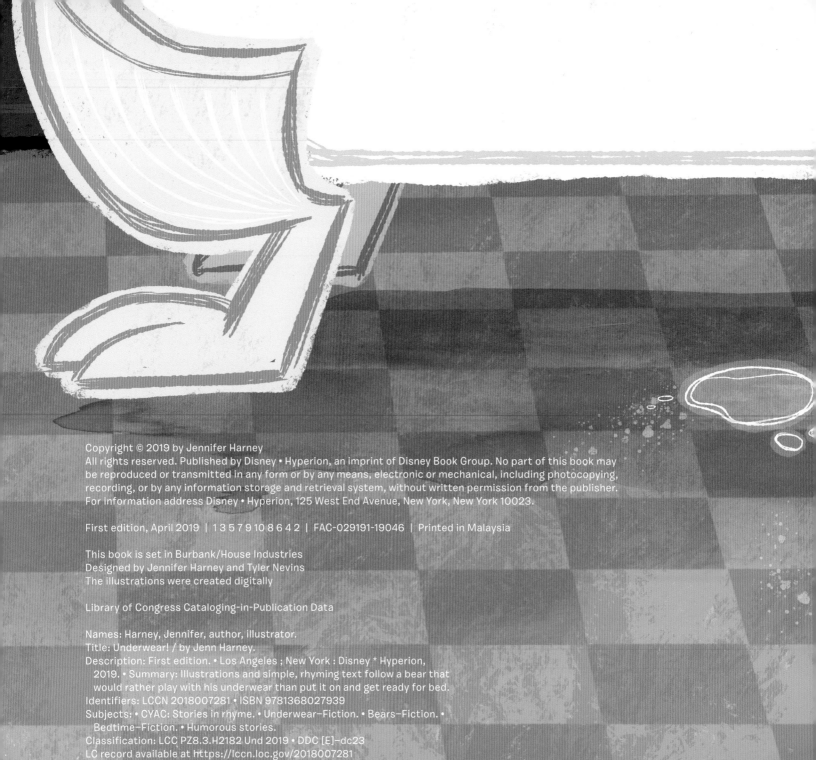

First edition, April 2019 | 1 3 5 7 9 10 8 6 4 2 | FAC-029191-19046 | Printed in Malaysia

This book is set in Burbank/House Industries
Designed by Jennifer Harney and Tyler Nevins
The illustrations were created digitally

Library of Congress Cataloging-in-Publication Data

Names: Harney, Jennifer, author, illustrator.
Title: Underwear! / by Jenn Harney.
Description: First edition. • Los Angeles ; New York : Disney * Hyperion,
    2019. • Summary: Illustrations and simple, rhyming text follow a bear that
    would rather play with his underwear than put it on and get ready for bed.
Identifiers: LCCN 2018007281 • ISBN 9781368027939
Subjects: • CYAC: Stories in rhyme. • Underwear–Fiction. • Bears–Fiction. •
    Bedtime–Fiction. • Humorous stories.
Classification: LCC PZ8.3.H2182 Und 2019 • DDC [E]–dc23
LC record available at https://lccn.loc.gov/2018007281

Reinforced binding

Visit www.DisneyBooks.com

For Roy and Peg

Bare
Bear. . .

"Here's a spare."

Where to wear this underwear?

DOWN
here?

Underwear makes awesome hair.

And goggle-wearing AQUABEAR!

Lights go **OUT.**

I'll *dive* in there.

BEWARE, Big Bear—
Here comes...

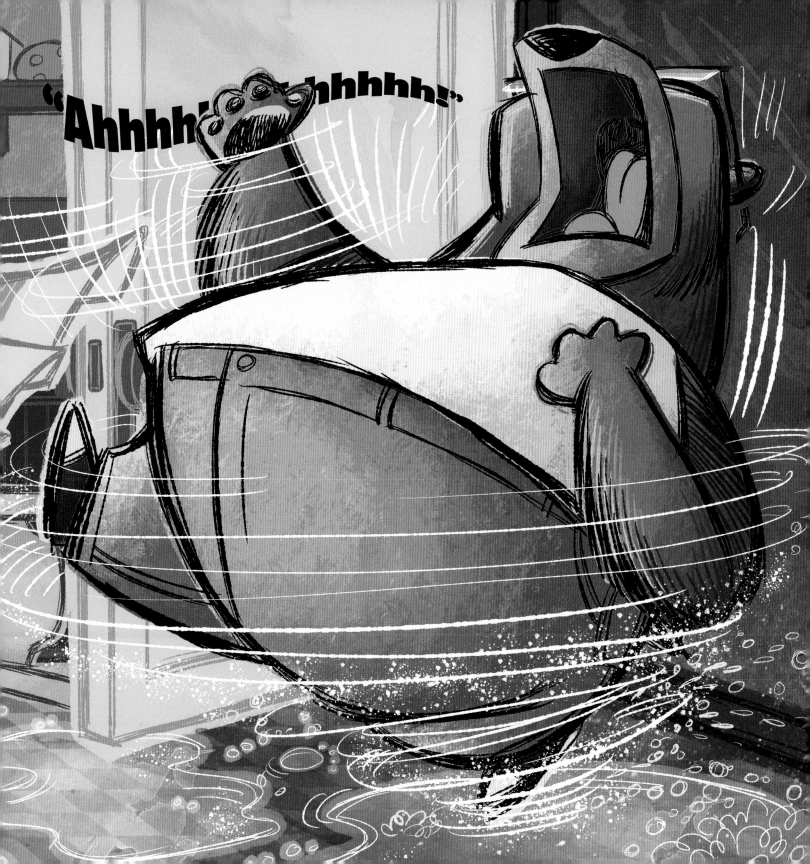

Go and grab a dry new pair."

"Underwear?"

**"Well,
time for bed,
I do declare!"**

tiptoe tiptoe tiptoe tiptoe tiptoe tiptoe tiptoe tiptoe tiptoe tiptoe tiptoe tiptoe tiptoe

"Sleep tight, sweet bear,
snugly tucked in under there."